Children's Books:

Princess Charlotte and the Pea

Sally Huss

Princess Charlotte and the Pea

"If there is one thing a princess should be,

It is to have the quality of sensitivity.

She must be SENSITIVE!"

That is what the prince had demanded…

And that is what Jacob had been commanded.

Yes, the prince had told him,

"Find a sensitive girl to be my wife,

One I can live with happily all my life."

So Jacob went to work stacking mattresses.

He stacked mattresses upon mattresses and still more mattresses.

This was a tough job that he'd been assigned –

A true princess he had to find.

He had devised a simple plan

That he had been using throughout the land

Of hiding a tiny pea

Beneath stacks of mattresses so that he could see…

Which girl would be sensitive enough to feel it.

And when he'd find her, she would be <u>IT.</u>

She would be the princess he had been looking for

And his long search would be no more.

He had gone to one village after another.

Girls were brought in by fathers, mothers, even a brother.

In each village he had stacked mattresses up high

And then let each of the town's girls give it a try.

She had to try to feel something as small as a pea hidden deep

within the stack.

If she could, he would take her back --

Back that is to the castle to meet the prince.

This was a foolproof test that he had created. This was a cinch.

So on this day, Jacob stacked and stacked and when he was done
He again secretly slipped a pea between two mattresses with his
fingers and thumb.

Then he helped each prospective princess climb the ladder.

When she lay on top, he yelled, "Lie a little flatter."

Spread eagle she lay there. He hoped she'd sense the pea.

"I feel nothing," she called down. "It must not be me."

She climbed back down with a saddened face

And faced the others with some disgrace.

"Next," called out Jacob. "Keep moving along."

Up went another girl. The line was still long.

"Are you lying there," Jacob asked, "as flat as can be?"

"Yes," she answered. "But I can't feel a thing. It must not be me."

Down she came and another went up to the top.

He wondered when his search for a princess would ever stop.

"I feel a little something," he could hear the third girl call.

"This is very uncomfortable. It feels like a ball.

Is there a ball of some kind beneath one of the mattresses?"

"Oh, oh," sighed Jacob. He hoped she wasn't one of those actresses

Who had tried to lie their way into the race

By trying to take a real princess's place.

"No. Now that I really feel it, it's not that big,"

Called the girl from the top of the mattress rig.

"It could be a pea that I feel."

"Oh my, oh my," cried Jacob, "a princess for real!"

"Come down. Come down. I need to take you to the castle."

He was happy that he was now at the end of this hassle.

"Goodbye, dear family and friends," waved the princess-to-be

Charlotte Divine.

They waved back, happily calling out, "Have a fine time."

Jacob helped her up on his horse-drawn carriage

"Thank you," said Charlotte, "for helping with my future marriage."

Jacob and Charlotte rode away in his over-stuffed wagon

With the mattresses piled on top, a little bit saggin'.

When they arrived at the castle gate, it was very, very late.

Off to bed Charlotte was escorted.

"In the morning," she was told, "your new life will be

properly sorted."

"Goodnight," said Jacob to the princess-to-be.

"I'm glad you're the one who sensed the pea."

"Goodnight, kind Jacob," said Charlotte so sweetly.

"Tomorrow," said Jacob, "everything will be arranged quite neatly."

So the princess-to-be slept on a bed with no pea.

She slept soundly and happily, not knowing what would be.

In the morning a rush of attendants washed her and dressed her

And even a priest came to the castle and blessed her.

She was now ready to meet the prince.

There was nothing about her that the prince could take offense.

She was fed and cleaned and dressed to the gills

In ribbons and pearls and taffeta frills.

When the prince arrived, all stood at attention.

Charlotte spoke first, "There is something I need to mention.

I feel if there is one thing a prince should be –

It is to have the quality of sensitivity.

He must be SENSITIVE!"

The crowd found her comments somewhat provocative.

"But," said the prince. "I am a prince already, my dear.

"In that case," explained Charlotte, "you have nothing to fear."

"Jacob," she called, "bring out the mattresses and let's see what he sees."

Then she whispered in Jacob's ear, "Don't let him see, but hide

two peas."

So once again, Jacob stacked the mattresses way up high.

They practically poked a hole in the sky.

After hiding the peas, he helped the prince climb the ladder

And whispered to him, "It works best if you lie flat, even better if
you lie flatter."

Once on top, the prince lay down.

"Do you feel anything?" Charlotte inquired from the ground.

"I feel a little something, a tiny, little mound. In fact there seems to be two."

"That will do," said Charlotte. "That will do."

When the prince returned,

Charlotte said, "Still, it's not enough to be sensitive enough

to feel a pea.

No. No, that's not good enough for me.

Who among all these people have you slighted?

When you have corrected that, then I will consider you as knighted."

The prince thought a moment, then gave Jacob a glance.
Oh yes, he hadn't thanked Jacob when he had the chance.

He hadn't thanked him for finding the girl who would be

his princess for all time –

The lovely and kind Charlotte Divine.

After apologizing and thanking Jacob…

The prince sank to his knees,

Then turned to Charlotte and asked,

"Will you be my princess, please?"

"Perfect," said Charlotte, now happy to be

The bride of one so filled with sensitivity.

A prince or a princess is one who is sensitive and kind,

One who knows what is on another's mind,

And can ease their burden with a word or a glance,

Can raise their spirit and make their heart dance.

It is not necessary that he or she wear a crown.

In everyday people such a person can be found.

The end,
but not the end
of being kind
and sensitive
to the feelings
of others.

At the end of this book you will find a Certificate of Merit that may be issued to any child who promises to honor the requirements stated in the Certificate. This fine Certificate will easily fit into a 5"x7" frame, and happily suit any girl or boy who receives it!

FREE GIFT

Receive a special Sally Huss children's e-book FREE by going to: http://www.sallyhuss.com/free.html.

Here are three more delightful "Princess" books by Sally Huss. They may be found on Amazon.

About the Author/Illustrator

Sally Huss

"Bright and happy," "light and whimsical" have been the catch phrases attached to the writings and art of Sally Huss for over 30 years. Sweet images dance across all of Sally's creations, whether in the form of children's books, paintings, wallpaper, ceramics, baby bibs, purses, clothing, or her King Features syndicated newspaper panel "Happy Musings."

Sally creates children's books to uplift the lives of children and hopes you will join her in this effort by helping spread her happy messages.

Sally is a graduate of USC with a degree in Fine Art and through the years has had 26 of her own licensed art galleries throughout the world.

This certificate may be cut out, framed, and presented to any child who has earned it.

Certificate of Merit

_____
(Name)

The child named above is awarded this Certificate of Merit for acting in a manner suitable of a prince or princess:

*By being kind and sensitive to the feelings of others

*By saying and doing things that make others happy

Presented by: _____   Date: _____